T0365371

for

Ian and Sean

To order additional copies of this book, contact:
Xlibris
1-888-795-4274
www.Xlibris.com
Orders@Xlibris.com

ISBN: 978-1-4134-8502-8 (sc)
ISBN: 978-1-4134-8503-5 (hc)

Library of Congress Control Number: 2005900750

Print information available on the last page

Rev. date: 05/21/2020

2

The Six Wives of Henry VIII

Lion = King   Griffin = England

JUNE 28 1491   JANVARY 28 1547

Text and illustrations

by

Sheilah Beckett

KING HENRY VIII

JUNE 28 1491

JANVARY 28 1547

KING HENRY VIII

Undoubted flower and very heir

of the two noble and illustrious

families of Lancaster and York

HENRY VIII

List to the tale of Henry Eight,

Of six ladies aspiring to share in his fate.

For the glory of England, for the conceit of the man,

No soul e'er denied him from the day he began.

Each whim, each demand, always met with obeisance.

All powerful, unquestioned a true man of the Renaissance.

CATHERINE
of ARAGON

All sweetness and light was Catherine of Aragon,

The groom was delighted his betrothed a paragon,

But weightier matters soon were at stake,

The dynastic succession, for the Tudor line's sake.

Then Mary arrived—not what he'd planned,

Yet surely next time, an heir for England.

But birth after birth brought Mary no brother,

Girls didn't count; Pa blamed it on Mother.

He divorced her for failing her prescribed obligations,

He would not be thwarted in his expectations.

CATHERINE
of ARAGON

9

1532 · HENRY VIII ✳ ANNE BOLEYN

10

ANNE BOLEYN

Anne Boleyn was a lady of breeding,

King Henry thought perfect for seeding,

So out went Catherine and bairn from court,

And in came Anne his new consort.

Though instead of an heir to the English throne,

Elizabeth appeared, causing Henry to groan.

Then rumors of Anne being smitten by Smeaton,

How dare the young hussy, his royal heart eaten

With fury, this cuckold king swore and erupted.

Keen axes, warm necks, two lives were disrupted.

ANNE BOLEYN

JANE SEYMOUR

*N*ow we couldn't agree more,

That pious Jane Seymour

Was reluctant to be whisked off to bed,

Yet was finally persuaded,

And in nine months elated

To present Hal her little son, Ed.

With pomp he's presented,

The succession cemented,

But it all was too much for poor Jane.

She expired without warning,

And was buried next morning

In Windsor, "His favorite" was lain.

JANE SEYMOUR

ANNE of CLEVES

Though Holbein strove mightily to please,

The portrait, alas, was no tease.

Plain Annie would simply not do.

Quel dilemma! Wise Anne quit her queenly claim.

Voila' a dependant "sister" became.

So now shelving Annie, the search renewed

Impatient Hal, fresh prospects viewed.

To refill the royal bed lonely

With a Queen, a fifth one-and-only.

ANNE of CLEVES

1540   HOWARD

HENRY VIII   ✳   CATHERINE

CATHERINE HOWARD

Anne Boleyn's cousin Catherine Howard,

Gay and curvatious and surely no coward,

Flirted and beguiled that wandering-eyed king,

Ignoring the perils of a May-December fling.

But the gap in the years, and the lack of a son,

For the besotted old man, and the chippy he'd won,

Soon made him impatient with his fun loving wife.

He list Cranmer's tattling, and vented his spleen,

For her indescretions she was conveyed to Tower Green.

An unfortunate end to a reckless life.

CATHERINE
HOWARD

CATHERINE PARR

An R. N. the only role that she had,

Pampering and babying that monstrous old cad.

Can't have been fun, but her duty she knew,

She gathered around her his family crew.

Mary, Elizabeth and Edward as well

As plain "Sister" Anne who came home to dwell.

Meanwhile the court continued to simmer,

Old Henry ignored it all, and grew dimmer.

Gout-ridden and feeble, the old despot departed.

Amen, sighed all England, few broken-hearted.

CATHERINE PARR

29

30

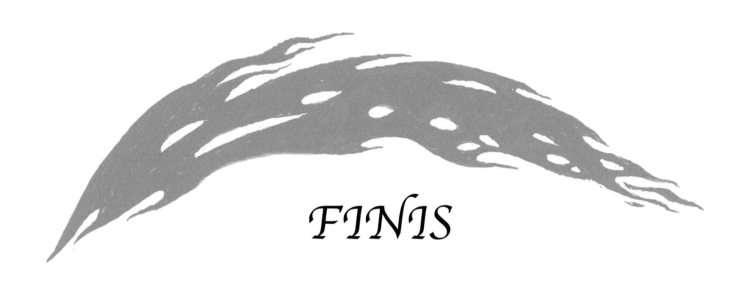

FINIS

And that is the saga of Henry Eight,

Lecher, or captain of his ship of state.

He married three Catherines two Annes and poor Jane,

Two beheaded, one banished, one shelved as too plain,

One died, and three siblings survived to be crowned,

But this infamous tyrant, this scholar renowned,

Had wound up his legend, had had his last say,

The Tudors and England must carry the fray.

Summon the mourners, and toll the bell,

Then leave him to Heaven, or more likely Hell.

Catherine of Aragon   Mary   Anne Boleyn

Queen 1509
Divorced 1533
Died 1536

Born 1516
Queen 1553
Died 1558

Queen 1533
Beheaded 1536

Elizabeth 1

Born 1533
Queen 1558
Died 1603

Jane Seymour

Queen 1536
Died 1537

Edward

Born 1537
King 1547
Died 1553

33

Anne · Catherine · Catherine

Anne of Cleves   Catherine Howard   Catherine Parr

Queen 1540   Queen 1540   Queen 1542
King's Sister 1540   Beheaded 1542   Widowed 1547

34

The Ravens live at the Tower of London.

Their wings are clipped so they cannot fly.

Legend has it that the Tower and the Empire

would fall should the Ravens disappear.

The Six Wives of Henry VIII

JUNE 28 1491

JANVARY 28 1547

Lion = King

Griffin = England

Printed in the United States
By Bookmasters